E   Martel, Cruz.
Mar   Yagua days

DATE DUE   PERMA-BOUND

Yagua Days

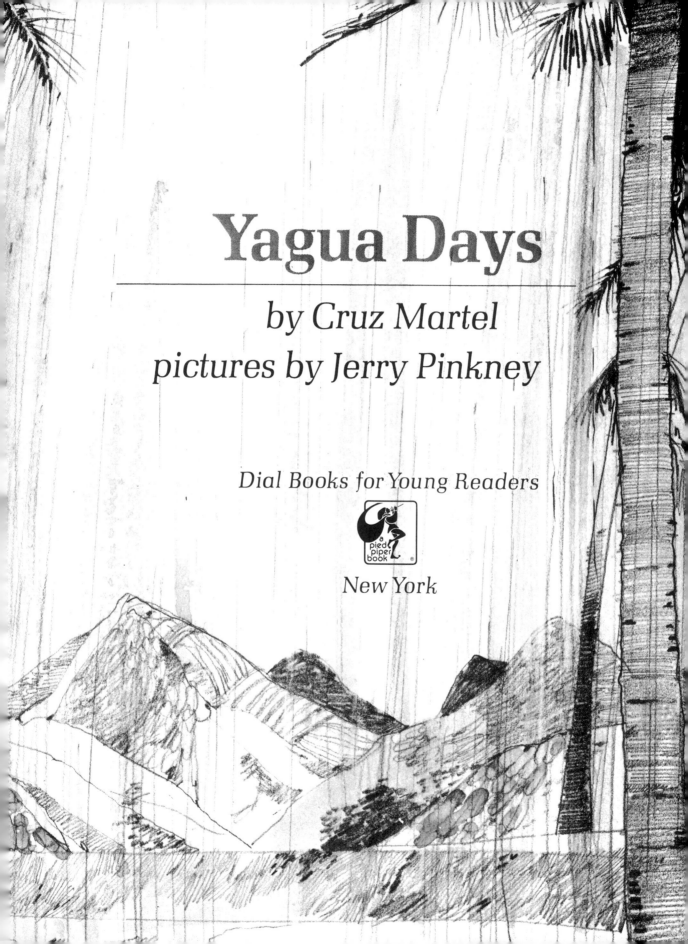

Yagua Days

by Cruz Martel
pictures by Jerry Pinkney

Dial Books for Young Readers

a pied piper book ®

New York

Published by Dial Books for Young Readers
A Division of Penguin Books USA Inc.
375 Hudson Street
New York, New York 10014

A Pied Piper Book is a registered trademark of
Dial Books for Young Readers,
a division of Penguin Books USA Inc.,
® TM 1,163,686 and ® TM 1,054,312.

YAGUA DAYS
is published in a hardcover edition by
Dial Books for Young Readers.
ISBN 0-8037-0457-7

At the back of this book you will find a
Spanish word list
that includes definitions and pronunciations.

para Mamá

It was drizzling steadily on the Lower East Side. From the doorway of his parents' bodega, Adan Riera watched a car splash the sidewalk.

School had ended for the summer two days ago, and for two days it had rained. Adan wanted to play in East River Park, but with so much rain about the only thing a boy could do was watch cars splash by.

Of course he could help father. Adan enjoyed working in the bodega. He liked the smells of the fruits and the different colors of the vegetables, and he liked the way the mangós, ñames, and quenepas felt in his hands.

But today he would rather be in the park. He watched another car spray past. The rain began to fall harder.

Mailman Jorge sloshed in, slapping water off his hat. He smiled. "Qué pasa, Adan? Why the long face?"

"Rainy days are terrible days."

"No—they're wonderful days. They're yagua days!"

"Stop teasing, Jorge. Yesterday you told me the vegetables and fruits in the bodega are grown in panel trucks. What's a yagua day?"

"Muchacho, *this* day is a yagua day. And Puerto Rican vegetables and fruits *are* grown in trucks. Why, I have a truck myself. Every day I water it!"

EXTRA
LONG GRA

Adan's mother and father came in from the back.

"Hola, Jorge. You look wet."

"I *feel* wetter. But it's a wonderful feeling. It's a yagua-day feeling!"

His mother and father liked Jorge. They had all grown up together in Puerto Rico.

"So you've been telling Adan about yagua days?"

"Sí. Mira! Here's a letter for you from Corral Viejo, where we all had some of the best yagua days."

Adan's father read the letter. "Good news! My brother Ulise wants Mami, Adan, and me to visit him on his finca for two weeks."

"You haven't been to Puerto Rico in years," said Mailman Jorge.

"Adan's *never* been there," replied his mother. "We can ask my brother to take care of the bodega. Adan will meet his family in the mountains at last."

Adan clapped his hands. "Puerto Rico! Who cares about the rain!"

Mailman Jorge smiled. "Maybe you'll even have a few yagua days. Hasta luego. Y que gocen mucho!"

Tío Ulise met them at the airport in Ponce.

"Welcome to Puerto Rico, Adan."

Stocky Uncle Ulise had tiny blue eyes in a round, red face, and big, strong arms, but Adan, excited after his first plane ride, hugged Uncle Ulise even harder than Uncle Ulise hugged him.

"Come, we'll drive to Corral Viejo." He winked at Adan's father. "I'm sorry you didn't arrive yesterday. Yesterday was a wonderful yagua day."

"You know about yagua days too, tío Ulise?"

"Sure. They're my favorite days."

"But wouldn't today be a good yagua day?"

"The worst. The sun's out!"

RANDOL ELEMENTARY

In an old jeep, they wound up into the mountains.
"Look!" said Uncle Ulise, pointing at a river jumping rocks. "Your mother and father, Mailman Jorge, and I played in that river when we were children."

They bounced up a hill to a cluster of bright houses. Many people were outside.

"This is your family, Adan," said Uncle Ulise.

Everyone crowded around the jeep. Old and young people. Blond-, brown-, and black-haired people. Dark-skinned and light-skinned people. Blue-eyed, brown-eyed, and green-eyed people. Adan had not known there were so many people in his family.

Uncle Ulise's wife Carmen hugged Adan and kissed both his cheeks. Taller than Uncle Ulise and very thin, she carried herself like a soldier. Her straight mouth never smiled—but her eyes did.

The whole family sat under wide trees and ate arroz con gandules, pernil, viandas and tostones, ensaladas de chayotes y tomates, and pasteles.

Adan talked and sang until his voice turned to a squeak. He ate until his stomach almost popped a pants button.

Afterward he fell asleep under a big mosquito net before the sun had even gone down behind the mountains.

In the morning Uncle Ulise called out, "Adan, everyone ate all the food in the house. Let's get more."

"From a bodega?"

"No, mi amor. From my finca on the mountain."

"You drive a tractor and plow on the mountain?"

Tía Carmen smiled with her eyes. "We don't need tractors and plows on our finca."

"I don't understand."

"Vente. You will."

Adan and his parents, Aunt Carmen, and Uncle Ulise hiked up the mountain beside a splashy stream.

Near the top they walked through groves of fruit trees.

"Long ago your grandfather planted these trees," Adan's mother said. "Now Aunt Carmen and Uncle Ulise pick what they need for themselves or want to give away or sell in Ponce."

"Let's work!" said Aunt Carmen.

Sitting on his father's shoulders, Adan picked oranges.

Swinging a hooked stick, he pulled down mangós.

Whipping a bamboo pole with a knife tied to the end, he chopped mapenes from a tall tree.

Digging with a machete, he uncovered ñames.

Finally, gripping a very long pole, he struck down coconuts.

"How do we get all the food down the mountain?" he asked.

"Watch," said Aunt Carmen. She whistled loudly.

Adan saw a patch of white moving in the trees. A horse with a golden mane appeared.

Uncle Ulise fed him a guanábana. The horse twitched his ears and munched the delicious fruit loudly.

"Palomo will help us carry all the fruit and vegetables we've picked," Adan's mother said.

Back at the house, Adan gave Palomo another guanábana.

"He'll go back up to the finca now," his father said. "He's got all he wants to eat there."

Uncle Ulise rubbed his knee.

"Que te pasa?" asked Adan's mother.

"My knee. It always hurts just before rain comes."

Adan looked at the cloudless sky. "But it's not going to rain."

"Yes, it will. My knee never lies. It'll rain tonight. Maybe tomorrow. Say! When it does, it'll be a yagua day!"

In the morning Adan, waking up cozy under his mosquito net, heard rain banging on the metal roof and coquies beeping like tiny car horns.

He jumped out of bed and got a big surprise. His mother and father, Uncle Ulise, and Aunt Carmen were on the porch wearing bathing suits.

"Vamonos, Adan," his father said. "It's a wonderful yagua day. Put on your bathing suit!"

In the forest he heard shouts and swishing noises in the rain.

Racing into a clearing, he saw boys and girls shooting down a runway of grass, then disappearing over a rock ledge.

Uncle Ulise picked up a canoelike object from the grass. "This is a yagua, Adan. It fell from this palm tree."

"And this is what we do with it," said his father. He ran, then belly-flopped on the yagua. He skimmed down the grass, sailed up into the air, and vanished over the ledge. His mother found another yagua and did the same.

"Papi! Mami!"

Uncle Ulise laughed. "Don't worry, Adan. They won't hurt themselves. The river is down there. It pools beneath the ledge. The rain turns the grass butter-slick so you can zip into the water. That's what makes it a yagua day! Come and join us!"

That day Adan found out what fun a yagua day is!

Two weeks later Adan lifted a box of mangós off the panel truck back in New York.

"Hola, muchacho! Welcome home!"

Adan smiled at Mailman Jorge. "You look sad, compadre."

"Too much mail! Too much sun!"

"What you need is a yagua day."

"So you know what a yagua day is?"

"I had six yagua days in Puerto Rico."

"You went over the ledge?"

"Of course."

"Into the river?"

"Sí! Sí! Into the river. Sliding on yaguas!"

"Two-wheeled or four-wheeled yaguas?"

Adan laughed. "Yaguas don't have wheels. They come from palm trees."

"I thought they came from panel trucks like mine."

"Nothing grows in trucks, Jorge. These mangós and oranges come from trees. The gandules come from bushes. And the ñames come from under the ground. Compadre, wake up. Don't *you* know?"

Mailman Jorge laughed. "Come, campesino, let's talk with your parents. I want to hear all about your visit to Corral

Spanish Word List

arroz con gandules (ah-ROHZ kon ghan-DOO-les) · rice with pigeon peas

bodega (boh-DEG-ah) · Puerto Rican grocery store

buenos días (BWEN-noss DEE-ahs) · good day or hello

campesino (kham-peh-SEE-noh) · country boy

compadre (kom-PA-dreh) · pal

coquies (koh-KEES) · tree frogs

Corral Viejo (koh-RALL vee-YEH-hoh) · old corral

ensaladas de chayotes y tomates (en-sah-LAH-dahs deh chah-YOH-tehs ee toh-MAH-tehs) · salads of avocados and tomatoes

finca (FEEN-kah) · plantation

guanábana (ghwah-NAH-bah-nah) · a sweet, pulpy fruit, slightly smaller than a football, covered with prickly skin

hasta luego (AH-stah loo-WEH-goh) · till we meet again; good-bye

hola (OH-la) · hello

mami (MAH-mee) · mommy

mangó (mahn-GO) · a sweet, tropical fruit, golden when ripe

mapenes (mah-PEN-nehs) · breadfruit

mi amor (mee ah-MOHR) · my love

mira (MEE-rah) · look

muchacho (moo-CHA-choh) · boy

ñame (NYAH-meh) · a tropical root vegetable similar to a potato

Palomo (pah-LOH-moh) · dove

papi (PAH-pee) · daddy

pasteles (pahs-TELL-ehs) · Puerto Rican dumplings

pernil (pehr-NEEL) · roast pork butt

plátano (PLAH-ta-noh) · a tropical fruit similar to a banana

qué pasa? (keh PAH-sah) · what's happening?

qué te pasa? (keh teh PAH-sah) · what's the matter?

quenepa (keh-NEH-pah) · a grape-sized fruit with a hard, green peel

sí (see) · yes

tía (TEE-ah) · aunt

tío (TEE-oh) · uncle

tostones (tohs-TOH-nehs) · fried green plantains

vámonos (BAH-moh-nohs) · let's go

vente (BEN-teh) · come on

viandas (vee-AHN-dahs) · general term for Puerto Rican vegetables

y que gocen mucho (ee keh GOH-sen MOO-choh) · and have fun!

yagua (JAH-gwah) · the outer covering of a sprouting palm frond